Granddaddy
Parallelogram
The Power of Unity

Janel Williams

To order additional copies of this book, contact:
Xlibris
1-888-795-4274
www.Xlibris.com
Orders@Xlibris.com

Acknowledgments

I thank all my friends and family for supporting me. I would like to especially thank my parents, Fred and Brenda Sherron; my sister, Melinda Carroll; and my sweet children, Shelia and Micah, for inspiring me to finish this book. Shelia and Micah, thank you for giving Mommy space to write this book. I love you dearly.

Introduction

I was intrigued by a study conducted by the University of Chicago entitled, "Math at home adds up to achievement in school." In this study, Berkowitz et. al states, "When parents and children interact about math story problems – even as little as once a week – children increased math achievement by the end of the school year." The study further suggests that students who are exposed to bedtime math stories approach math with less anxiety. This study inspired me to write the first of the Granddaddy Parallelogram series for my children.

The concept of Granddaddy Parallelogram and his family were originally created for my high school geometry students who struggled with remembering properties of parallelograms. After creating character names and characteristics for each parallelogram, I found that my high school students enjoyed learning geometry and remembered the facts with ease.

I expounded on the idea and developed a story for my young children. I was amazed to discover that my five-year-old son understood all the concepts just as well as my eleven-year-old daughter. My five year old began to share his knowledge of parallelograms with his teachers, and they were astonished by his ability to grasp these advanced concepts at such an early age. I then shared this story with my seventy-one-year-old mother, who always struggled with geometry, and she too was able to learn all the advanced geometric terms and concepts.

Now I want to share this story with others. My desire is for children to learn and love math early and to appreciate it throughout their lives.

Please visit CreativeIntelligentMe.com to find more creative math products and books for all ages.

Once there was a land called the Land of Quadrilaterals. It was a warm place where everything had four sides. The sun was a golden rectangle, the clouds were bright white diamonds, and the trees entailed brown rectangles and green rhombuses. The playgrounds, the schools, the houses, and, of course the polygons that lived there had four sides too! It was a great place to be, if you were a quadrilateral.

MAYOR

The most popular four-sided polygon that lived in the Land of Quadrilaterals was Granddaddy Parallelogram. He was the mayor of Parallelogram City. Granddaddy Parallelogram conducted most of his business in his home, but he was frequently distracted by his grandson, Rect the Rectangle, and granddaughter, Rhombella the Rhombus.

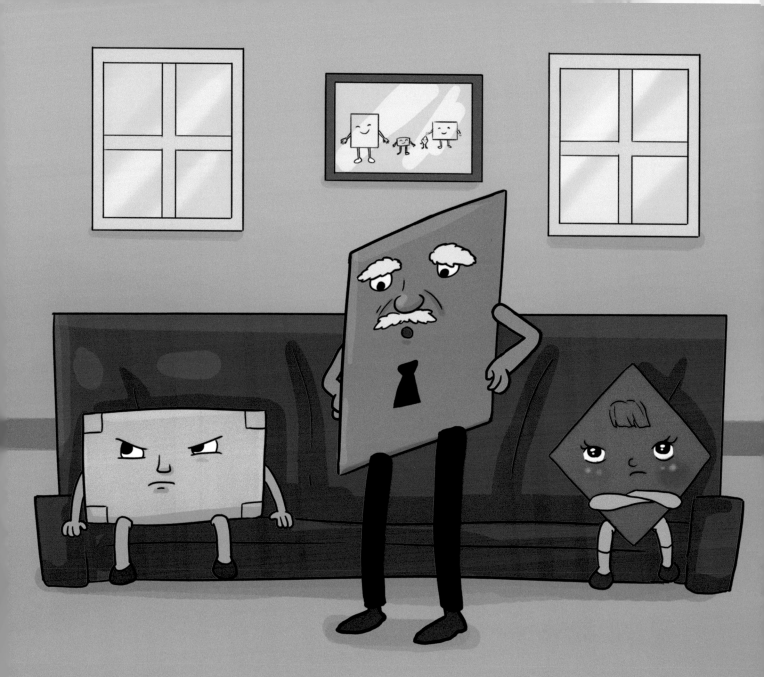

One day, Granddaddy Parallelogram came home and heard Rect and Rhombella arguing. "I wish there was a way to make them stop quarrelling," grumbled Granddaddy Parallelogram. Granddaddy Parallelogram was fed up with the noise and decided to call a family meeting.

Rect was sitting on one side of the couch, and Rhombella sat on the other. "Why do you feel you have to argue all the time?" asked Granddaddy Parallelogram.

"Rect brags about having four right angles," cried Rhombella. "He said he will always be smarter than me because he will always be right."

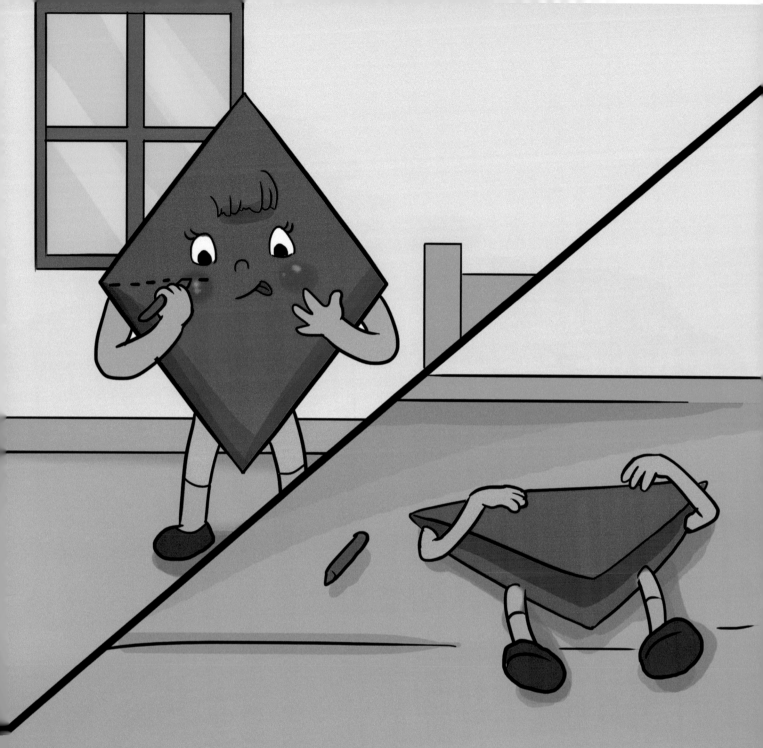

"Rhombella thinks she is more attractive than me because all her sides have equal lengths," replied Rect.

"Well, I can't help it if polygons think I am a beautiful diamond!" interjected Rhombella.

"She also brags about her cool trick," rejoined Rect. "She can fold her equal sides into one another and spin on an angle."

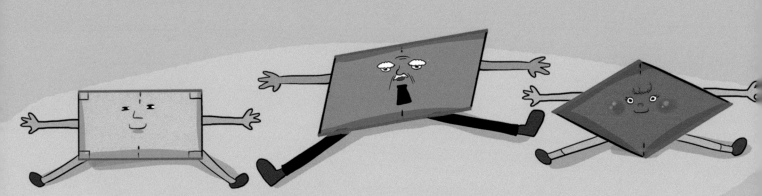

"Enough!" shouted Granddaddy Parallelogram. "You are both special. You both have unique qualities, like myself. Both pairs of your opposite sides are parallel. That means if you stretch your sides very high or very low, your opposite sides will not intersect. If you stretch to the left or right, the other opposite sides won't intersect either. Let's try it together," suggested Granddaddy Parallelogram.

Rhombella and Rect rose from their seats and stretched up and down, right and left. Rhombella and Rect discovered that their opposite sides will never cross, no matter how high or wide they stretched their sides.

They were both pleased with their discovery, but it did not stop Rhombella and Rect from arguing.

Rhombella left the family meeting upset and stomped to her bedroom. "I can't take this anymore," murmured Rhombella. "Being a pretty Rhombus, with all equal sides, is not enough. I want to be right, just like my brother Rect," declared Rhombella. "I deserve respect from my brother and others."

Rhombella walked over to her bedroom window and gazed at the moon and made a wish. "Oh please, oh please, let me be right. Make me smart on this bright, bright night." Rhombella continued to glare at the moon until she fell asleep.

The next day, Rhombella woke up to a bright, sunshiny day. She believed this was going to be the best day of her life. She got dressed quickly, grabbed her book bag, and ran out the door.

"Hi, Mr. Quad-mon," said Rhombella as she waved to the school's crossing guard.

As Rhombella approached the school's front door, she tripped on a rock and fell on her tummy. "Ouch!" shrieked Rhombella. Just then, her friends started to laugh, and she began to cry. "This is supposed to be the best day of my life! What happened?" she murmured.

As Rhombella rose from her fall, Rhombella took note of students staring at her with astonishment. The students gasped and declared, "Are those diagonals?"

Rhombella noticed her arms and legs were in an unfamiliar position! Her arms and legs crossed each other to form diagonals.

"OMG!" exclaimed Rhombella. "I have diagonals, and they are perpendicular. That means, when my diagonals cross, they form *right angles! I am smart too!*"

All the rhombuses in school began to mimic Rhombella's position and discovered they too had diagonals that were perpendicular.

Rhombella shook her legs and feet back in place and ran home to show Granddaddy Parallelogram and her brother Rect her novelty.

"Granddaddy, my wish has come true! Watch what I can do!"
Rhombella exclaimed eagerly. Just then, Rhombella displayed her
ability to cross her arms and legs to make them diagonals. "Look,
I have diagonals, and they are perpendicular. That means my
diagonals meet at right angles. I may not have right angles in
each of my corners, but my diagonals cross to form right angles.
Rhombuses are smarties too!" asserted Rhombella.

Rect gasped at what he was seeing. "Do I have the ability to create diagonals too?" asked Rect.

"Yes, you do," assured Granddaddy Parallelogram.

Just then, Rect sat on the floor, crossed his arms and legs, and created diagonals too. "I can't believe this," bellowed Rect. "I have diagonals too! My diagonals may not be perpendicular, but they are handsomely equal!"

"This is a great day," asserted Granddaddy Parallelogram. "You both are attractive and smart in your own special ways. Rhombella, you have pretty sides that are equal and smart diagonals that cross to form right angles!" exclaimed Granddaddy Parallelogram. "Rect, you have four right angles in each of your corners and diagonals that are handsomely equal!"

Rhombella and Rect smiled with joy.

"Now that you know this, I think it is time for the two of you to learn the greatest secret of all," stated Granddaddy Parallelogram. Just then, Rhombella and Rect experienced fright and excitement simultaneously.

"In order for you to learn this secret, you must promise me one thing," proclaimed Granddaddy Parallelogram.

"Sure! What is it?" asked Rect.

"You two must promise to stop fighting so that we can unite as a family." They both agreed.

"OK! The time has come," pronounced Granddaddy Parallelogram. "Let's hold hands." Rhombella and Rect grabbed Granddaddy's hand. "Now walk in a circle and repeat after me," instructed Granddaddy Parallelogram. "We will not fight, we must unite. We will not fight, we must unite. We will not fight, we must unite."

Rhombella and Rect followed Granddaddy's instructions, and after the third time, the most amazing thing happened!

The ground began to tremble, kitchen dishes began to fall, and the sun became brighter.

No one could have guessed what happened next! POOF! Rect and Rhombella gasped as they saw the most precious little creature appear.

"Yes! Yes!" harked Granddaddy Parallelogram. "The old history books were correct. When a parallelogram, rectangle, and rhombus unite, a precious square is formed."

"Wow!" exclaimed Rhombella. "Does that mean all squares are parallelograms, rectangles, and rhombuses at the same time?"

"Yes!" said Granddaddy Parallelogram. "See what happens when you stop fighting and start uniting? There is great power in unity."

More parallelograms, rectangles, and rhombuses continued to recite the unity rhyme; and more precious squares were formed. And the Land of Quadrilaterals became an even better place to live.

THE END!

Parent/Teacher Tips

While this book is intended to be an enjoyable fairy tale, it is also created to expose young children to basic and advanced math vocabulary and concepts. Therefore, this book's design affords an opportunity to read it as literature and to teach mathematical concepts. Allow your young scholars to lead you.

Repetition is critical for children to retain information. Try to include this book in your child's reading list at least twice a month. The math geek notes are for the teacher or parent who desires to understand math at a deeper level. A parent may choose to share these notes with their child.

Keep math enjoyable and reinforce the concepts by applying the following suggested steps:

After Page 1

Ask: What is a quadrilateral? *(Children will understand from context clues.)*
Possible answers: A quadrilateral is a closed shape with four sides or a four-sided polygon.
Activity: Allow children to walk around the room and point to objects that are quadrilaterals.
Math geek note: A quadrilateral is technically two-dimensional (flat) and not three-dimensional. So when a child points to a mirror, etc., let them call it a quadrilateral, but touch one side of the mirror as they call it a rectangle, square, etc.

After Page 3

Ask: What does Rect the Rectangle keep bragging about?
Answer: He has four right angles in each of his corners and thinks he is smarter than Rhombella because he is always right.

After Page 5

Ask: What is true about Rhombella the Rhombus?
Answer: She has four beautiful equal sides. Since all her sides are equal in length, they can fold neatly into one another.
Activity: Give children copies of printed rhombuses. Instruct them to fold the rhombuses so that all the equal sides meet.
Math geek note: You should see that a triangle is formed, but don't mention it unless the child brings it up. The goal is to stress that a rhombus has four equal sides.

During/After Page 6

Activity: Have the children get out of their seats and do the exercise with Granddaddy Parallelogram. Stress that if the sides were stretched really high or low, opposite sides will never intersect (cross). Remind them that this is called parallel.
Now have the students stretch their arms to the left and right, while pointing to the diagram in the book, and show opposite sides will not intersect (cross) either.
Ask: What is true about both pairs of opposite sides of a parallelogram?
Answer: Opposite sides are parallel. That means the bottom and top sides won't ever cross and the left and right sides won't cross either.
Math geek note: It is important to point out that all members of the family have opposite sides that are parallel. Therefore, everyone can do the exercise. (This makes them all parallelograms.)

After page 11

Ask: What did Rhombella and other rhombuses discover about their diagonals? Make sure you point to the diagonals and the four right angles that are formed.
Answer: Rhombella noticed that her diagonals are perpendicular, which means that when her diagonals cross, they make four right angles.

After Page 13

Ask: What did Rect the Rectangle discover about his diagonals?
Answer: They were equal in length.

After Page 18

Ask: How was a square formed?
Answer: A square was formed by uniting a parallelogram, rectangle, and rhombus.
Math Geek note: A parallelogram has opposite sides parallel, opposite sides equal in length, diagonals that bisect one another, and opposite angles that are equal.
A rectangle is a parallelogram with four right angles and diagonals that are equal.
A rhombus is a parallelogram with equal sides and perpendicular diagonals.
A square is a parallelogram, rectangle, and rhombus at the same time. Therefore, it has every property of each shape.

After book is read:

Activity: Play "Who Am I?"
State: I am a quadrilateral with four right angles. *Answer: Rectangle.*
State: I am a quadrilateral with four right angles and four equal sides. *Answer: Square.*
State: I am a quadrilateral with equal sides. *Answer: Rhombus.*
State: I am a quadrilateral with both pairs of opposite sides parallel. *Answer: Parallelogram.*
Activity: Have children draw a parallelogram, rhombus, rectangle, and square. Have them explain what they have in common and what makes them different.

Math Vocabulary

Diagonal - a line segment joining two opposite corners of a polygon.

Intersecting lines - lines that lie in the same plane (flat surface) and cross at exactly one point.

Parallel lines - lines that lie in the same plane (flat surface) and never intersect. They are always the same distance apart.

Parallelogram *(par-uh-lel-uh-gram)* - a quadrilateral with both pairs of opposite sides parallel.

Perpendicular lines- lines that intersect to form right angles.

Polygon - a closed flat shape that has three or more straight sides and angles.

Quadrilateral *(kwod-ruh-lat-er-uhl)* - any four-sided polygon.

Rectangle - a quadrilateral with four right angles.

Rhombus *(rum-bus)* - a quadrilateral with all four sides having equal length.

Square- a quadrilateral with four right angles and all four sides having equal length.

Printed in the United States
by Baker & Taylor Publisher Services